Dear Reader—

One of the greatest pleasures in my life is reading with my children, Jack and Romy. Each time we open a book together, we are transported to a new adventure, a fresh perspective, or a magical encounter. The pictures and printed words not only offer a worthwhile story, but provide a gateway to a personal conversation that we share.

When I watch my children as we read—them wide-eyed and engrossed in the pages— I find myself energized by their hunger to discover new things and humbled that I can participate in the intimate experience of seeing them grow and learn before my very eyes.

This is the interaction between children and adults that is at the heart of Jumpstart's Read for the Record.

Through this campaign, Jumpstart will engage thousands of citizens across America in reading with a child to bring the experience of one-to-one reading to all children.

I hope you will join me in reading *The Little Engine That Could* to a young child in your life. Your participation will strengthen a connection with a child you love and will also support Jumpstart's efforts to unlock the potential in all of America's children.

Just by purchasing this book, you have already made a difference, as the proceeds from each copy support one hour of the Jumpstart program delivered to a young child at risk of failing in school.

So, Read for the Record for you, for your child, and for every child in every city and town in our country. Thank you for joining us as we work toward the day when every child in America enters school prepared to succeed.

Best,

Matt Lauer

WELCOME TO JUMPSTART!

Thank you for purchasing this special edition of *The Little Engine That Could* and for participating in Jumpstart's Read for the Record, a celebration of the caring relationships between young children and adults, who together enjoy the excitement and benefits of reading.

Sadly, many of America's children miss out on these reading relationships and enter kindergarten unprepared, even though research demonstrates that quality early learning experiences at home and preschool can set at-risk children on a path for school success, increase their chances of graduating high school and even reduce their chances of becoming involved in crime.

For the Record . . . Too Many Children Enter School Unprepared to Learn

In the United States today, as many as 35 percent of children enter our schools without the skills needed to succeed.

Shockingly, in our nation's low-income communities, children receive as few as 25 hours of one-to-one reading time by age 5, while their middle-income peers are read to as many as 1,700 hours by age 5. As a result, these low-income children enter first grade with one-fourth the vocabulary of their middle-income peers.

For the Record . . . Jumpstart Helps Children Thrive

Jumpstart is a national nonprofit organization that has worked with children from low-income communities since 1993 to prepare preschoolers for kindergarten—one child at a time. At 65 colleges throughout the country, 2,500 college students each work one-to-one with a preschool child who is in danger of entering kindergarten behind his or her peers.

For the Record . . . You Can Help

Please help us Read for the Record to advance early education opportunities for every child and to directly support the children, families, and communities that Jumpstart serves each year.

Read *The Little Engine That Could* to a child and set the world record at home or at one of the many events nationwide. Registration is free and will be followed with a certificate of participation. Each registration earns Jumpstart $1 from a generous donor.

Register and learn more at: www.readfortherecord.org

Through Jumpstart's Read for the Record, participants across America will join Jumpstart to set a world record and spread the power of shared learning.

iii

jumpstart

HOW TO READ WITH A YOUNG CHILD
Jumpstart Tools for Making the Most of Reading Time

The following tips are based on proven reading techniques developed by experts and adapted by Jumpstart. While regular reading is very important, simple techniques—like the ones listed below—can increase the quality of the learning experience and expand the benefits.

Begin Early
The journey to becoming readers, writers, and learners begins when babies are born. Years of playing, talking, listening, and reading together become the foundation for social and literacy skills necessary for success in school and life.

Reading with your child every day is a wonderful way to:
- Help your child learn about letters and new words.
- Give your child time to practice speaking and listening.
- Encourage lifelong positive attitudes toward reading.
- Increase your child's knowledge and understanding of his or her own community, other places in the world, and other cultures.

Make Reading a Conversation
- The conversations you have before, during, and after reading are just as important as the actual reading.
- Read often. Establishing a pattern for reading gives a child confidence in your relationship.
- Take turns reading and let your child ask and respond to questions.
- Take turns sharing new words and information.
- *Your goal is to have the child become the teller of the story!*

Making Shared Time More Fun and Effective
While engaging your child in a conversation about this or any book:
- Listen to what your child says to find out more about your child's knowledge and interests.
- Build on your child's ideas by introducing new words and information.
- Point out aspects of the pictures, and encourage your child to talk about them.
- Point to each word as you read it; this helps your young child begin to make sense of the printed page.
- Ask your child one or two questions per page that begin with the words *what, where, when, why,* and *how,* and wait for a response. Questions that ask for more than a yes-or-no answer encourage conversation and comprehension skills.
- Follow your child's lead: If he or she wants to talk about a particular picture or idea, stay with it! You do not need to read every word on the page to make it a meaningful reading experience.
- Talk about what happened in the story after you have read it.
- Have fun with the story—make sound effects and read with great enthusiasm!

A CONVERSATION WITH YOUR YOUNG READER
ABOUT *THE LITTLE ENGINE THAT COULD*

The Little Engine That Could is a wonderfully re-illustrated classic picture book through which you can create an enjoyable and enriching experience for a young child. Here are some examples for reading together based on the tips from the previous page.

So Many Toys　　After reading pages 8-9, point to the airplane and say, "I think this airplane is something you could take a ride in to visit someone. What else could you ride in to visit someone?" Wait for your child's response. Repeat the child's idea and add more information. For example, Child: "A car." Adult: "You could ride in a car. I also think you could ride in a bus like we did when we went to the park to see the turtles."

The Big Strong Engine　　After reading pages 20-21, point to the picture of the little broken-down engine and say, "How do you think the little engine is feeling?" Wait for your child's response and then say, "Why do you think the little engine is feeling that way?"

　　Point to the other engine. Then say, "Do you remember what this kind of engine is called?" Wait for your child's response. Then add ideas such as, "It is called a Freight Engine. This Freight Engine is loaded with big machines for printing books and newspapers." Wait to hear if your child has anything to add to the conversation. Then turn to the other engines and initiate a conversation about each of them.

"I think I can—I think I can—I think I can"　　While pointing to the words on page 38, say, "I think I can—I think I can—I think I can" and invite your child to say the words with you. Then have some fun repeating the words together by saying them faster and louder, imitating a train's puffing.

　　Refer to the pictures and say, "Wow, the Little Blue Engine looks like it is working very hard to get up the mountain. How do you think such a little engine gets up that big mountain? Do you remember doing something that seemed very hard? How did you do it?"

Learn more reading tips online at www.readfortherecord.org

THE LITTLE ENGINE THAT COULD

This book is dedicated to my mother, Elizabeth Long,
who knows something of climbing mountains   —L. L.

TO THE READER

She would start with a soft whisper . . . I think I can, I think I can, I think I can. Slowly her voice would grow . . . I think I can, I think I can, I think I can. Until finally with a resolute confidence, she'd read, . . . I think I can, I think I can, I think I can.

Even today as an adult, a father myself, I can still hear my mother's voice and that familiar cadence as she would read those powerful words to me. I can see the rocking chair we would sit in together in my bedroom, and I still feel the warmth of those moments.

Though multitudes of people have read *The Little Engine That Could,* spanning many generations, when I was a young boy it seemed to have been written and created only for me. It was my book, it was my story and it was my message.

I loved the spunk of Little Blue and her willing determination has inspired and actually sustained me in some pretty harrying instances throughout my life.

I'm comforted by the knowledge that my grandma read *The Little Engine That Could* over and over to my mother all the way back in the 1940s when she was a little girl. My mother then read it to me time and time again when I was little. I have now read it to my little boys over and over again. And one day, perhaps, my two sons will read *The Little Engine That Could* again and again to their own children . . . my grandkids.

THE LITTLE ENGINE THAT COULD

retold by
Watty Piper

with new art by
Loren Long

PHILOMEL BOOKS   *in association with* GROSSET & DUNLAP

Chug, chug, chug. Puff, puff, puff. Ding-dong, ding-dong. The little train rumbled over the tracks. She was a happy little train for she had such a jolly load to carry. Her cars were filled full of good things for boys and girls.

There were toy animals—giraffes with long necks, Teddy bears with almost no necks at all, and even a baby elephant. Then there were dolls—dolls with blue eyes and yellow curls, dolls with brown eyes and brown bobbed heads, and the funniest little toy clown you ever saw.

8

And there were cars full of toy engines, airplanes, tops, jack-knives, picture puzzles, books, and every kind of thing boys or girls could want.

But that was not all. Some of the cars were filled with all sorts of good things for boys and girls to eat—big golden oranges, red-cheeked apples, bottles of creamy milk for their breakfasts, fresh spinach for their dinners, peppermint drops, and lollypops for after-meal treats.

The little train was carrying all these wonderful things to the
good little boys and girls on the other side of the mountain.
   She puffed along merrily.

Then all of a sudden she stopped with a jerk. She simply
could not go another inch. She tried and she tried, but her wheels
would not turn.

What were all those good little boys and girls on the other side of the mountain going to do without the wonderful toys to play with and the good food to eat?

"Here comes a shiny new engine," said the funny little clown
who jumped out of the train. "Let us ask him to help us."

So all the dolls and toys cried out together:

"Please, Shiny New Engine, won't you please pull our train

over the mountain? Our engine has broken down, and the boys and girls on the other side won't have any toys to play with or good food to eat unless you help us."

But the Shiny New Engine snorted: "I pull you? I am a Passenger Engine. I have just carried a fine big train over the mountain, with more cars than you ever dreamed of. My train had sleeping cars, with comfortable berths; a dining-car where

waiters bring whatever hungry people want to eat; and parlor cars in which people sit in soft arm-chairs and look out of big plate-glass windows.

"I pull the likes of you? Indeed not!"

And off he steamed to the roundhouse, where engines live when they are not busy.

How sad the little train and all the dolls and toys felt!

Then the little clown called out, "The Passenger Engine is not the only one in the world. Here is another engine coming, a great big strong one. Let us ask him to help us."

The little toy clown waved his flag and the big strong engine came to a stop.

"Please, oh, please, Big Engine," cried all the dolls and toys together. "Won't you please pull our train over the mountain? Our engine has broken down, and the good little boys and girls on the other side won't have any toys to play with or good food to eat unless you help us."

But the Big Strong Engine bellowed: "I am a Freight Engine. I have just pulled a big train loaded with big machines over the mountain. These machines print books and newspapers for grown-ups to read. I am a very important engine indeed. I won't pull the likes of you!"

And the Freight Engine puffed off indignantly to the roundhouse.

The little train and all the dolls and toys were very sad.

"Cheer up," cried the little toy clown. "The Freight Engine is not the only one in the world. Here comes another. He looks very old and tired, but our train is so little, perhaps he can help us."

So the little toy clown waved his flag and the dingy, rusty old engine stopped.

"Please, Kind Engine," cried all the dolls and toys together.

"Won't you please pull our train over the mountain? Our engine has broken down, and the boys and girls on the other side won't have any toys to play with or good food to eat unless you help us."

But the Rusty Old Engine sighed: "I am so tired. I must rest my weary wheels. I cannot pull even so little a train as yours over the mountain. I can not. I can not. I can not."

And off he rumbled to the roundhouse chugging, "I can not. I can not. I can not."

Then indeed the little train was very, very sad, and the dolls

and toys were ready to cry.

But the little clown called out, "Here is another engine coming,
a little blue engine, a very little one, maybe she will help us."

The very little engine came chug, chugging merrily along.
When she saw the toy clown's flag, she stopped quickly.

"What is the matter, my friends?" she asked kindly.

"Oh, Little Blue Engine," cried the dolls and toys. "Will you pull us over the mountain? Our engine has broken down and the

good boys and girls on the other side won't have any toys to play with or good food to eat, unless you help us. Please, please, help us, Little Blue Engine."

"I'm not very big," said the Little Blue Engine. "They use me only for switching trains in the yard. I have never been over the mountain."

"But we must get over the mountain before the children awake," said all the dolls and the toys.

The very little engine looked up and saw the tears in the dolls' eyes. And she thought of the good little boys and girls on the other side of the mountain who would not have any toys or good food unless she helped.

Then she said, "I think I can. I think I can. I think I can." And she hitched herself to the little train.

She tugged and pulled and pulled and tugged and slowly, slowly, slowly they started off.

The toy clown jumped aboard and all the dolls and the toy animals began to smile and cheer.

Puff, puff, chug, chug, went the Little Blue Engine. "I think I can—I think I can—I think I can—I think I can—I think I can—I think I can—I think I can—I think I can—I think I can."

Up, up, up. Faster and faster and faster and faster the little
engine climbed,

until at last they reached the top of the mountain.

Down in the valley lay the city.

"Hurray, hurray," cried the funny little clown and all the dolls and toys.

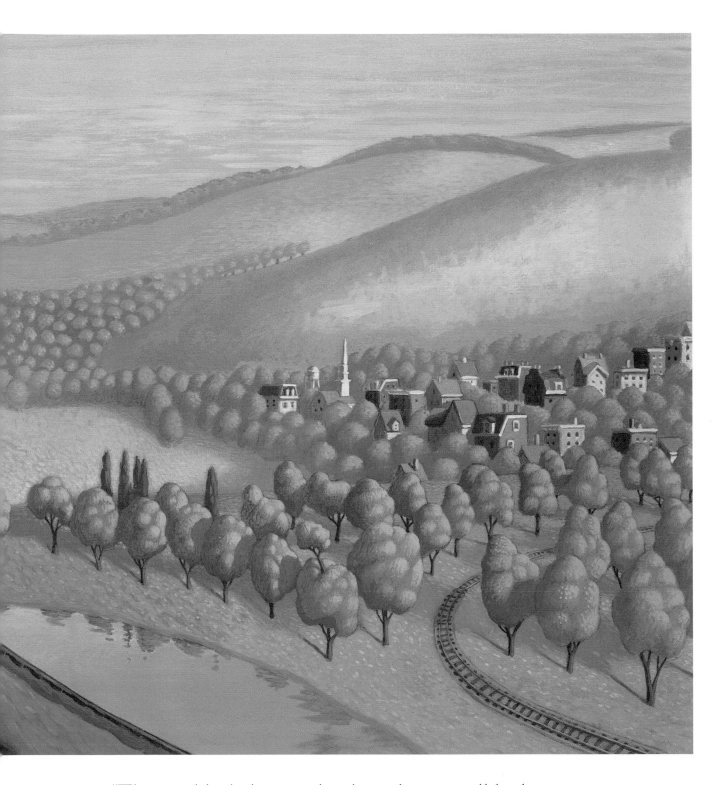

"The good little boys and girls in the city will be happy
because you helped us, kind, Little Blue Engine."

And the Little Blue Engine smiled and seemed to say as she puffed steadily down the mountain, "I thought I could. I thought I could. I thought I could. I thought I could. I thought I could. I thought I could."

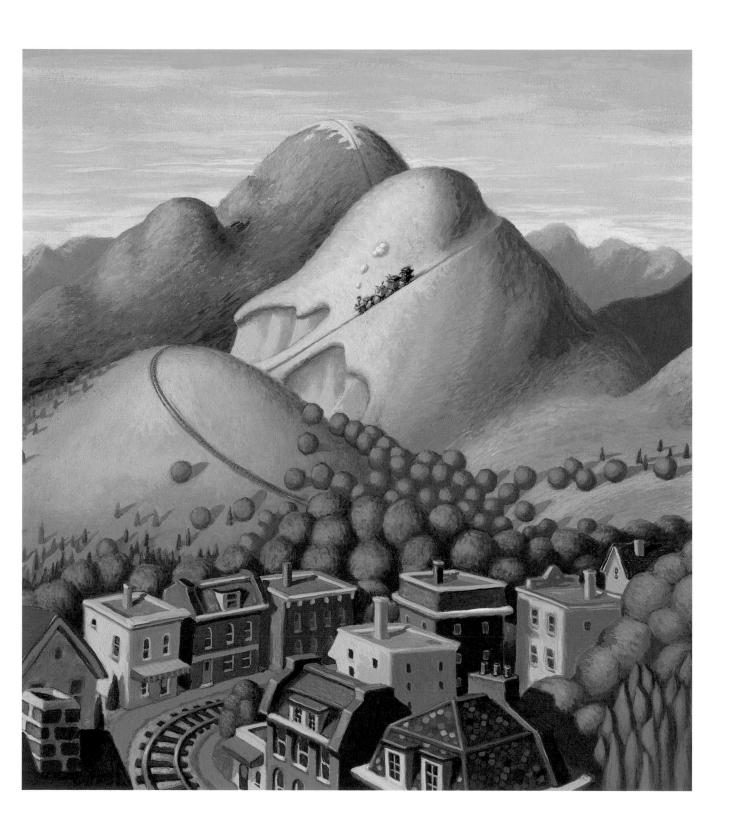

*Special thanks to Patti Gauch for sharing her wisdom and enthusiasm, to Semadar Megged for her
dedication and for being herself, to Doug Whiteman for his confidence in me,
and to Nicholas Callaway for his vision. —L.L.*

PATRICIA LEE GAUCH, EDITOR

Illustrations by Loren Long.

PHILOMEL BOOKS
in association with GROSSET & DUNLAP
Divisions of Penguin Young Readers Group.   Published by The Penguin Group.
Penguin Group (USA) Inc., 375 Hudson Street, New York, NY 10014, U.S.A.
Penguin Group (Canada), 10 Alcorn Avenue, Toronto, Ontario, Canada M4V 3B2 (a division of Pearson Penguin Canada Inc.)
Penguin Books Ltd, 80 Strand, London WC2R 0RL, England.
Penguin Ireland, 25 St. Stephen's Green, Dublin 2, Ireland (a division of Penguin Books Ltd.)
Penguin Group (Australia), 250 Camberwell Road, Camberwell, Victoria 3124, Australia (a division of Pearson Australia Group Pty Ltd).
Penguin Books India Pvt Ltd, 11 Community Centre, Panchsheel Park, New Delhi - 110 017, India.
Penguin Group (NZ), Cnr Airborne and Rosedale Roads, Albany, Auckland 1310, New Zealand (a division of Pearson New Zealand Ltd).
Penguin Books (South Africa) (Pty) Ltd, 24 Sturdee Avenue, Rosebank, Johannesburg 2196, South Africa.
Penguin Books Ltd, Registered Offices: 80 Strand, London WC2R 0RL, England.

Design by Semadar Megged.   Text set in 20-point Pastonchi.   The illustrations are rendered in acrylic.

Library of Congress Cataloging-in-Publication Data
Piper, Watty, pseud.   The little engine that could / retold by Watty Piper ; with new art by Loren Long.   p. cm.
Summary: Although she is not very big, the Little Blue Engine agrees to try to pull a stranded train full of toys over the mountain.
[1. Railroads—Trains—Fiction. 2. Toys—Fiction.] I. Long, Loren, ill. II. Title.   PZ7.P64Li 2005   [E]—dc22   2004030496

ISBN 0-399-24650-9
1 3 5 7 9 10 8 6 4 2
First Impression

The Little Engine That Could is one of the most popular and famous children's books of all time. Over the years, it has sold many millions of copies. This newly illustrated edition is based on "The Complete, Original Edition," retold by Watty Piper and illustrated by George and Doris Hauman, originally published by Platt and Munk, now part of the Penguin Young Readers Group. Over the years, its title and its refrain of "I think I can" have become a permanent part of the American vernacular.

Loren Long graduated with a BA in Graphic Design/Art Studio from the University of Kentucky, and pursued graduate-level studies at the American Academy of Art in Chicago. He has received numerous accolades for his fluid WPA painting style, including two gold medals from the Society of Illustrators in New York, and the prestigious Golden Kite Award.

Long is the illustrator of many celebrated picture books for children, including Madonna's *Mr. Peabody's Apples*, *The Day the Animals Came* by Frances Ward Weller, and *I Dream of Trains* by Angela Johnson.

Loren Long lives in a Cincinnati suburb with his wife and two sons.

To learn more about the artist and his work, visit his website at www.lorenlong.com